SWEET PEA

SWEET PEA

A Black Girl Growing Up in the Rural South

JILL KREMENTZ

Foreword by Margaret Mead

Harcourt, Brace & World, Inc.   New York

Curriculum-Related Books, selected and edited by the School
Department of Harcourt, Brace & World, are titles of general
interest for individual reading.

First edition

Library of Congress Catalog Card Number: 71-88109

PRINTED IN THE UNITED STATES OF AMERICA

Foreword

Jill Krementz has drawn for us a portrait of Sweet Pea, a young
black girl who lives in Montgomery County, Alabama, in a
dilapidated house owned by "some people in Detroit."
Her camera illuminates the particular circumstances of Sweet
Pea's life—many of them strange to city and country children
in other parts of the United States. But Sweet Pea and her
brothers and sisters share the hopes and fears, the delights
and disappointments of American children everywhere,
at home, at school, at church, at Christmas. Americans
everywhere, adults and children, know what it is like to get a
whole family dressed at once and will chuckle over Jerry,
who lost his own shoe and insisted his mother's would do.
Every child who feels that his home isn't quite what he sees on
television will sympathize with Sweet Pea's wish for a house
with running water and a bed for each of her brothers. And
every child who has had a happy Christmas will share her
happiness at the end of the day when each of the children got
a "wheel," for which their mother had saved all year.

The third quarter of the twentieth century has seen a
tremendous widening of peoples' knowledge of each other as
photographs, films, and television have presented vivid
pictures of how other people live. And today all of us,
wherever we live, have the task of bringing our children closer
to people in other towns and states and nations, on the six
continents and the islands of the seas. This book will help.

But Jill Krementz has also given us a picture of a particular
child with a quality of joyousness all her own—who, in spite
of some sad and frightening dreams, feels she would be
happy if she were just in the twelfth grade.

MARGARET MEAD

August 21, 1969

I don't know where I got the name Sweet Pea but that's what everyone's called me for just about as long as I can remember. Some people call me Barbara—like some of my teachers and Reverend Ross.

I was born at home. A midwife named Mrs. Dollrong came and Mama paid her twenty-five dollars. She charges thirty-five now.

Mama says she's not going to have any more children because eight is enough, but that if she did she'd have them at home, because she'd just be too sick worrying about all of us if she went off to the hospital like she did when Jerry was born. They make you stay for three days and three nights.

I think I'd rather have my children in the hospital when I get old and have them. That's if I get married. I don't know yet if I want to get married when I grow up. But if I do I think he should be handsome.

Maybe I'd like it if he were a doctor. I'd like to have four children — two boys and two girls. I don't have a boyfriend. Anthony Tremble took me to a dance at school called the Coronation Ball and I wore my new yellow dress. My brothers teased me but Mama made them stop.

We all went — Mama and Junior and Lee and Lester and Jerry. Jerry wore his new shoes except he didn't dance because he's only three. My sister Peggy was there too. She doesn't live at home any more because she stays over at Mary Charles' house. But she comes home a lot and sometimes I walk over to see her when I have nothing to do or when I get mad at my brothers.

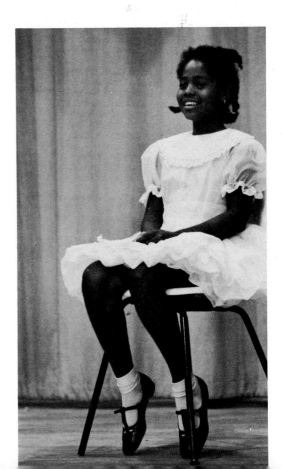

Peggy's my best friend even if she is my sister, and
we tell secrets to each other and laugh a lot. She took
me to a movie once in Montgomery. It was about

Ray Charles. I don't remember what it was called
because it was a long time ago, but I liked it and I wish
I could go again.

Emma and Minnie have been to the movies lots of times. They're my other two sisters, who don't live here any more. Emma is twenty and she's living in Atlanta now with Rodney and Joanne—they're her two children. She waits on tables at the bus terminal. She went to the Job Corps last year in Maine and learned how to be a cashier, but I guess she likes doing what she's doing better.

My other sister is Minnie and she's nineteen. She goes to Alabama State College and she comes home sometimes, but not as often as Emma. She writes to me, though. She was adopted by my uncle in Birmingham and the government pays for her school. I want to go to college too, except I want to go to Tuskegee. I don't know why.

If I had three wishes I would —

   Go to New York
   Be an airline stewardess

and I don't know any more — oh, I know —

   Be in twelfth grade.

When you're in elementary school you can't do anything.
In twelfth grade you get to go to parties and have
dances with boys.   I wouldn't mind boys if I was
in the twelfth grade.

We all go to the same school—Georgia Washington—except Jerry. He stays next door. I'm in the fourth grade. I get up about six and get myself ready.

Then Mama plaits my hair. It takes about a minute or two when she's going fast, but when she's going slow it takes a very long while. Then she leaves for work. She cooks at Penson's Restaurant and has to be there very early, so she leaves around seven o'clock. I can cook bacon and grits by myself, so I fix breakfast for everybody after she leaves.

Sometimes I brush my teeth—when I remember. I saw a dentist once, when I was in kindergarten. He came to our school and told us we should brush our teeth every day. When I was little, if I lost a tooth I would leave it under my pillow and the fairy would come and leave me a dime.

If I have time before the bus comes, I like to read or
study my lessons.   I like to read all kinds of books.
My favorite is "The Pony Tail That Grew."   It's about
a girl—her name was Betty—and every girl she saw had
a pony tail.   Even her doll that she got for Christmas
had a pony tail.   And so did her little sister.   But
she didn't have one.   She always wished for one and
one day she got sick and her hair started to grow long
and her mother fixed her a pony tail.   And everyone
came to her birthday party and gave her presents.

Sometimes I have a birthday party but last year I
didn't.   I was ten on October 25th and all I got was a
licking from my brothers.   I'd rather have an Easy
Bake than a licking.

The bus comes around eight, and we go outside and wait because it only stops for a minute. Our bus driver's name is Walter and he's been our bus driver since September. Junior misses the bus more than we do and has to walk, but when this happens a teacher usually picks him up.

The name of our principal is Mr. Williams, and he rings a bell every morning when it's time for us to go to our classes.

My homeroom teacher is Miss Wyman and the first thing she does is call the roll.

Then we pledge allegiance to the flag and pray and
sometimes we have an assembly.

I study arithmetic, language, science, social studies,
music, and physical education.   My favorite subjects
are spelling and social studies, but I like the other ones
all right.

In social studies we studied about Japan.   They grow
a lot of rice there and they eat it with chopsticks.   My
teacher Miss Saltzman brought some chopsticks to
school and showed us how to use them.   I want to
study to be an airline stewardess so I can travel a lot.
I'd like to go to Japan, New York, California, Miami,
Maine, and San Francisco.

We get a report card every six weeks and I get all
A's and B's, mostly A's.   I don't ever get any C's.

The other day we were talking about the first settlers who were in the state of Alabama. There were two Indians whose names were Pushmataha and Tecumseh, and Tecumseh wanted to fight the white settlers but Pushmataha didn't. Tecumseh got all the Indians around the campfire and he told them that they should fight, and then Pushmataha got up and told them about all the suffering and dying that would come from the war. He said that the new settlers had helped them with better ways of farming and had made the Indians richer with trade and had taught the Indian children how to read and write and the women how to keep better homes and that they shouldn't have a war.

My uncle's in Vietnam. He's been there a long time. People shouldn't fight. They should love one another. God said they should.

I like music because we get to sing and play instruments. I made a tambourine out of bottle caps and a clothes hanger.

We usually have physical education in our classroom, unless it's very warm and we can go outside. We have a new gym, but only older kids get to use it. It was only finished last year and Mr. Williams is very proud of it. They play basketball there, and they use it to rehearse plays. Peggy's in tenth grade so she gets to use it. That's where we had the Coronation Ball, but that's the only time I've been inside.

We have a basketball team that plays other schools. Mr. Williams wishes we could have a football team, but that would cost too much money because you have to pay for the equipment, and you also have to pay money to a coach and referees and for insurance.

You get a lunch ticket by paying thirty cents, or if your name is on a special list you get it for free. I don't have to pay. I like the lunches except I don't like coleslaw or snap beans or butter beans. We get regular milk with our lunch and we can buy chocolate milk if we want to, but it costs a dime so I don't get to buy it very often. And when I do, I don't drink it anyway because I bring it home to Jerry.

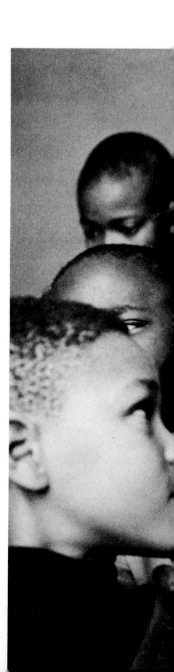

There are thirty-one in my section when nobody's absent but that never happens because some people are always sick or else they just don't come.

After lunch we have more classes and then we have to
clean up the room before we go home.   Around three
o'clock we start getting our books together and we sit
and wait for the bell to ring, and the minute it rings we
all run out to the buses.   Walter's bus is the first to
leave so I just start running as fast as I can.

First thing I do when I get home is say hello to
Pup-Pup, who's always waiting for the bus.

We usually get home before Mama does so we keep ourselves busy. I bring in the water from the well outside. I have to bring in enough for doing the dishes and for taking our baths after dinner. Lee chops the wood and brings it inside so we can start the fire for warming the kettle. Junior feeds the pigs. We have five now—a big one and four babies. We had more but Mama sold them at Christmas. She got twenty dollars for the big one and five dollars each for some babies. And two of the babies died. We've had pigs for as long as I can remember. I think they're funny looking.

Lester and Jerry are too little to help, so they just play.

Some days my Daddy comes to see us.   He comes
every other Thursday and his name is Henry Anderson.
He lives at Wild Bend and he works at the Vestry
Hospital taking patients into the operating room.
I went to a hospital once when I was about five or six
years old, because I was sick.   That's the only time I've
ever been to a doctor.   I only remember it a little bit.
   I don't remember when my father stopped living
here but I wish he still did, because I miss him.   Most
of the times he gives us all money and I save mine for
church, or else maybe I give it in at school—like when
we were seeing which class could raise the most amount
for the Coronation Ball.   He gives Mama fifteen
dollars every week for food and clothes.

Sometimes I go for a walk with Pup-Pup. I don't walk anywhere special. Sometimes I walk over to Mr. and Mrs. Pinkston's house to visit or to bring the rent money from Mama. Every month she pays Mr. Pinkston eighteen dollars, and he sends it to some people in Detroit because they own the house.

As soon as Mama gets home she starts fixing dinner, and she feeds Jerry because he's always wanting something to eat. Sometimes I help her—I set the plates and the cups on the table and pour the punch.
  I like pork chops and bologna and smoked sausage and potato salad and strawberry jello and grape drink best of all, but I like everything. And I like sweet-potato pie and chocolate cake. My Mama makes everything taste good—especially potato salad.

Before we start in eating, we say our verse.
If we forget, Mama asks us, "Did I hear you
say your verse?"—and whoever didn't say it
stops eating and says it then.   We each say
our own.   I say:

> God is great, God is good,
> And we thank thee for this food.
> By his hand we must be fed—
> Give us, Lord, our daily bread.

If I'm in a hurry I just say, "I was glad
when they said, let us go into the house of
the Lord."

After dinner we wash up. Lee
helps me or sometimes Junior, or
else they all run outside and play
and I do them alone. I'd rather
sweep than do the dishes.

43

Sometimes after dinner I like to play the flute.   Or if
my friend Barbara Willis walks over we jump rope.

Then maybe my Granddaddy comes over to visit.
He and Mama talk about church, and he asks us what
we've been doing and if we're going to come to the
farm on Saturday.

When my Grandmother died, I went to the funeral,
but there were so many people I had to stay in the car.
I felt sad. I miss her. She could be in heaven now.

We take our baths just about every night except when it's too cold.   Jerry always jumps in first.   Mama pours the hot water in and tells him to hurry on up, but he's

so bad and I just start bathing him. I say, "Jerry, will
you sit up and stop saying soap's in your eye," and he
just keeps on complaining that it's burning.

Then Lester and Lee and Junior take their tubs, and Jerry goes right on being bad until Mama picks up the switch she keeps over the fire and tells Jerry he's going to get a whopping.

He starts running away very fast. He thinks Mama won't catch him but she catches him if she wants to.

I like taking baths.   I took a bath in a real bathtub
once, when I was down to the Pinkstons' and I was
spending the night.   I like a real bathtub better
because it's bigger and you can move around.   I've
never taken a shower.

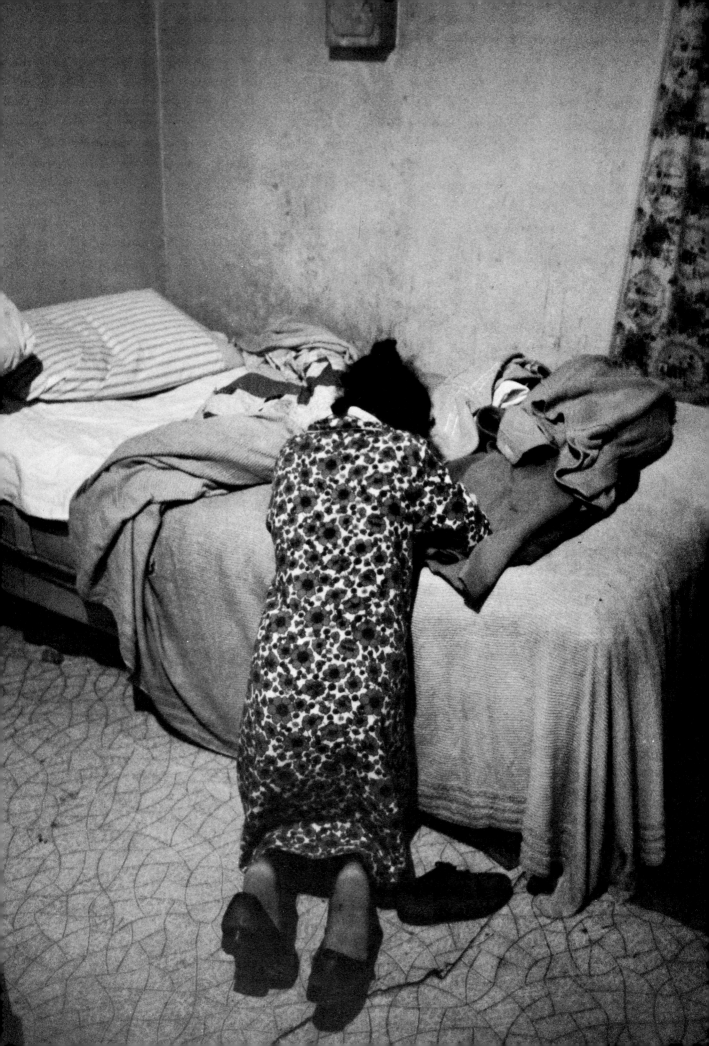

When I finish bathing myself I put on my nightclothes and then I say my prayers.   Sometimes if I need something—like when I need a new dress—I ask God for it.

Or maybe I ask Him to buy my Mama a new house. It would be brick and it would have four rooms like we have now, and it would have a heater in each room instead of fireplaces, so the house would heat up very quickly.

And there would be a bathroom with a tub and a sink.   And I would have a mirror in it.   And a window.   Oh I forgot—and a toilet.   We wouldn't keep the one outside any more.   I'd probably tear it down and fill the hole with dirt.

In the kitchen I'd have a stove, a refrigerator, a sink, a cabinet, and a table.   And I'd have running water in the sink.

I'd have six beds and my brothers would sleep in one, and Emma in one, and Peggy in one.   I'd save the rest for company.   I'd still sleep with my Mama, but maybe Jerry would sleep alone so we wouldn't have so many extra beds.

I think God is all colors.   That's what they said on the radio—that he doesn't have any special color.   If I drew a picture of Jesus, I'd put some light brown on him.   And I'd put some pink on him too.

We all go to bed at seven.   My brothers sleep in their room.

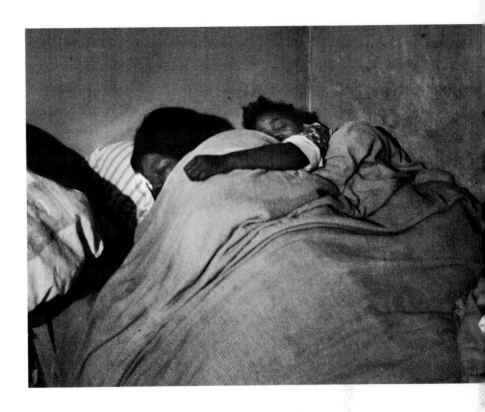

I sleep with my Mama in her room.   Sometimes
I dream about faraway places.   They're in wonderland
and I wish I could go there.   Most times I have bad
dreams and sometimes they wake me up, like someone's
going to get me.   I wake up before they get me.
Sometimes I cry when I have this kind of dream, but I
don't wake up my Mama.   I don't hardly have any
good dreams.

On Saturday Mama goes to work just like on the other
days.   I like to walk to the store if Mama asks me to
pick her up something, and Mrs. Harrison always says,
"Why hello there, Sweet Pea, and what can I do for you
today?"   She always asks after my Mama and the rest
of the children.   If I have any money left I buy some
peppermints because that's my favorite kind of candy.
My second favorite kind is buttermint.

When my Mama gets home she takes us in the car over
to my Granddaddy's farm.   That's where I like best of
all.   He gave me my own cow named Betty and one
day he showed me how to milk her.   First we had to
drag the calves away.   I was scared because I had
never milked a cow before, but it feels all right.

   I used to have a doll named Betty, but I didn't know
my cow when I had my doll and my Granddaddy didn't
know I had a doll named Betty.   In a way I do and in
a way I don't still like dolls.   I think I'm too old for
them now.

One time we caught some fish. First of all we sent Jerry
back up to the house to get a jar, and then Lee dipped
it down into the water and the fish went in and he
brought the jar up.   We didn't see the fish, so we
started to pour the water back, but then we looked in
again and saw two little baby ones.

We showed them to my Granddaddy and my Mama,
and after that Lee took them to school with him.   His
teacher has an aquarium, so Lee put them in there.

I like rolling down the hill
because I think it's lots of fun.

And I like climbing trees.

And I like going down to the pond too.   They used
to baptize people down there.   I never saw it, but
my Granddaddy's told me about it.   At church they
baptize in a little pool out back.   You wear a white
gown and they dip you down into the water.   It's not
very cold.

The preacher holds your nose and carries you back
over the water.   He's on one side and another man's
on the other side.   They do one at a time.   Sometimes
they baptize ten, sometimes twenty.   It's sort of like a
big day, and we go every year.   I was seven when they
baptized me.

My Granddaddy taught me how to pick cotton.   I
learned how to chop it by watching the other people.
I've been hoeing a row since I was eight.

They plant in March—they have machines to do that.
Then you chop it.   Then you plow it again and wait
until the last of August or the first of September and
then you pick it.

After you finish picking, the farmer weighs it on a
scale in a cotton sack—the same sack that you pick it
in.   A sack will hold about a hundred pounds.   If
you're a good cotton picker you can pick about
two hundred pounds in a day.   Mama can pick two
hundred pounds.   I can pick about forty pounds a day.
You get paid three pennies a pound.   It used to be
two pennies a pound.

Then there's a second picking, and the third picking
is called scrapping.   When you're scrapping they give
you four pennies a pound, because it's slower.

Picking it is worse than hoeing it.   Picking it, you're
stooping over all day, and hoeing you're standing up.
But I get blisters on my fingers from the hoe.   You
wear a lot of clothes to keep the sun off you.

Last year they made it against the law for children to
work in the cotton fields during school time.

When I get back from the farm, I like to go and visit
Peggy at Mary Charles' house and watch television.
We have one, but it doesn't work.   I like to watch
"Julia" the best.   And "Eye Guess."

Peggy has a lot of records and she lets me play them.
My favorite singers are Diana Ross and the Supremes,
Clarence Carter, and Aretha Franklin.

Sometimes I talk on Mary Charles' telephone — to
Louella Goldstein or to Darlene McDaid.   We don't
have a phone and most of my friends don't either.
I guess I've talked on a phone about fifteen times.
I liked it.

There's always a lot of people over at Mary Charles'
house.   Mrs. Murphy is always there — she lives just
down the road.   She's seventy-three years old and she's
worked in the cotton fields all of her life.   I like to
watch her dip snuff.

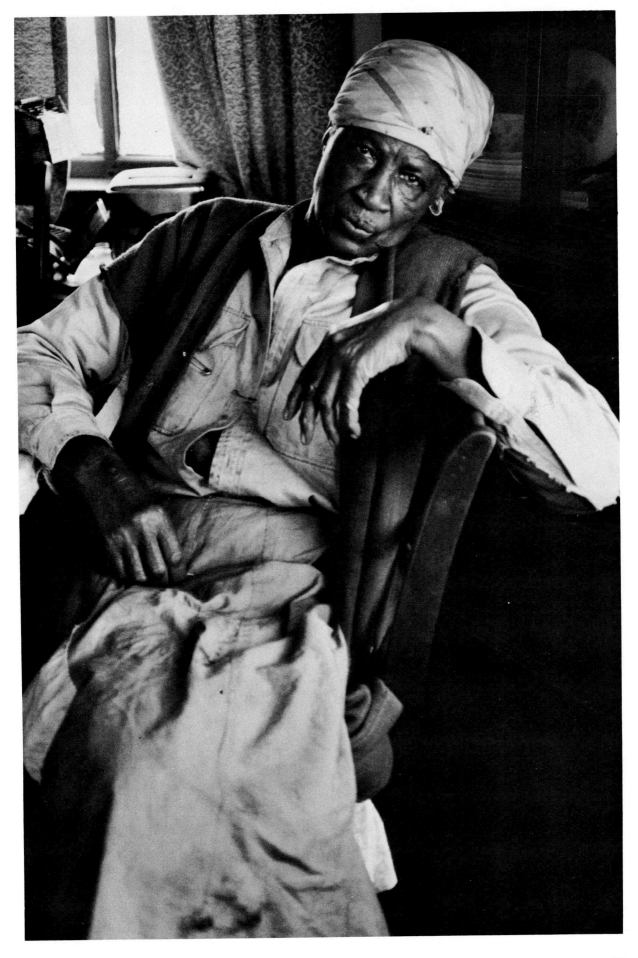

Peggy and I go to choir practice, and Thelma
McWhorter comes by to pick us up.   She's the lady
who plays the piano, and she rehearsed us when we
had a State Pageant.

Everyone was a different state—I was Texas and Peggy
was Hawaii and Myra was Illinois. You see which state
can get the most money, and whoever gets the most
is the winner. I got $1.30, because my Daddy gave
me a dollar and I sold some candy bars for the rest.

You walk down the aisle and tell the lady sitting there
how much you have, and she writes it down, and
everyone says "Amen" and "Praise the Lord" or whatever
they feel like saying—and then she adds it all up and
says how much money there is.

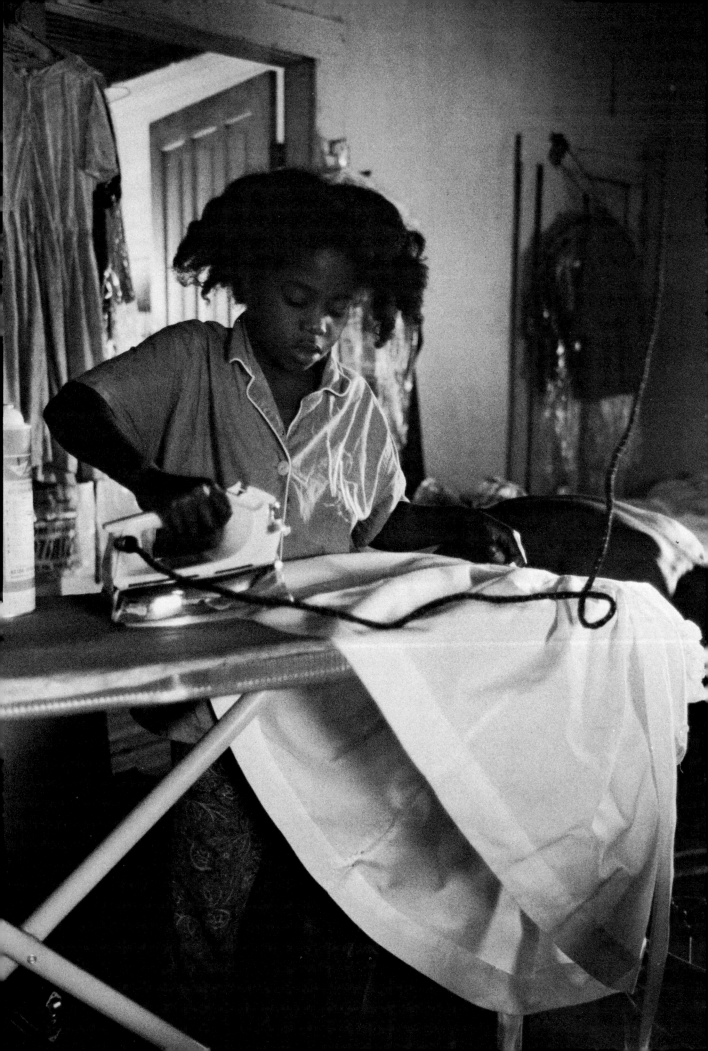

On Sunday we get up very early because we have to get
ready for church.   And there is a lot to do.
   One time Jerry lost his shoes.   We had to look all
over for them and we didn't get there until after the
meeting had started.   He said he would wear one
of Mama's shoes instead.   He is so bad.

Mama gets us ready first.

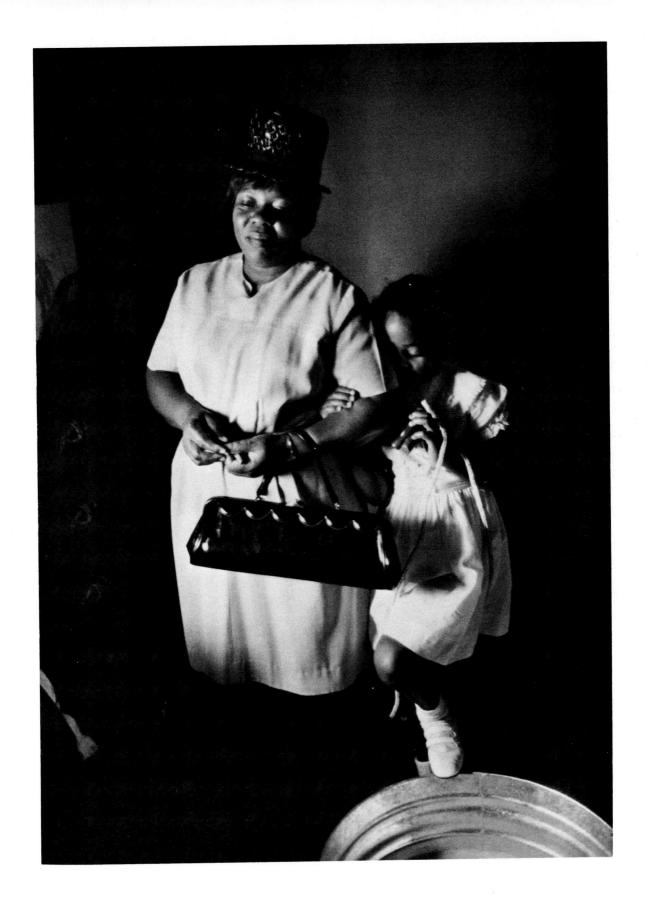

Then she puts on her hat and gets her purse.

At church we sing and we pray and Mama is an usher.
I like the preaching and the singing, but I like the
singing the best.

I've been in the Junior Choir for four years.
I don't have a favorite hymn but I like "Leaning
and Depending on Jesus."

When they take up the collection, Reverend Ross
says a prayer over the money.

Reverend Ross tells good stories. My favorite is the one about when Jesus told that man Jonah to go and tell the people about Him but he wouldn't go. He got in his boat and God sent a storm down on the sea and the captain of the ship got mad at Jonah for all the trouble he was causing. So Jonah got up and asked God to stop the rain and stop the storm. He stopped it. The captain asked God what did God want and God said there was a man on the boat He wanted. And I think Jonah jumped off the boat and the whale swallowed him and threw him up on the sand, and when he saw God he was afraid. I forget the end of it.

Jerry always falls asleep on the bench. He gets tired because he's been in church all day.

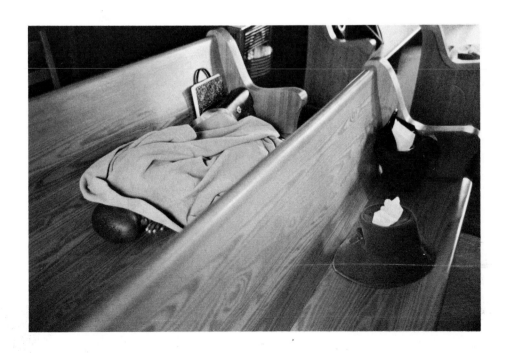

Some days we take Communion.

My Granddaddy is a deacon, and after we take
communion I shake hands with him, because he
stands next to Reverend Ross in the line.

After church gets out, we stand around and talk. Matilda Brown wears a penny on her leg to keep the pain away. It works on the wrist too.

About once a month we go and see my cousins, Emma May Moulton and her husband.

When we get home, maybe we play. But usually we just eat our Sunday meal and then we get ourselves ready for bed.

Of all the times of the year, I like Christmas best.
This year my Mama chopped down the Christmas tree
in the woods over by the church.   Lee and Lester went
with her and helped carry it home.
   We had the bulbs from last year, and Emma and I
fixed it up so it looked very pretty.

On Christmas night we put out the presents and the
oranges and candy, and I started to read the story
about Jesus being born, and Lee and Lester and Junior
sang "Silent Night" for the background.

Emma and I made the sweet-potato pie. She told me
if I kept on putting my hand in and tasting it, there
wouldn't be any left.

It was about the coldest night I can ever remember. Even Mama said she couldn't remember when it had ever been so cold. There was frost out on the porch and we had to keep the fire going all the time. Junior and Lee had to go outside and chop some more wood so there would be enough. When Emma was in Maine, she saw snow all the time. I've seen it a few times but there wasn't very much and it didn't last. Emma told me it looks pretty but it feels like ice if you stay in it for very long. But I still think it would be fun to play in it and I'd like to build a big snowman.

Mama told us we'd better get to bed because Santa wouldn't be dropping in till after we were all asleep. So we all went to bed.

Joanne was so sleepy that she fell asleep on the chair by the fire.

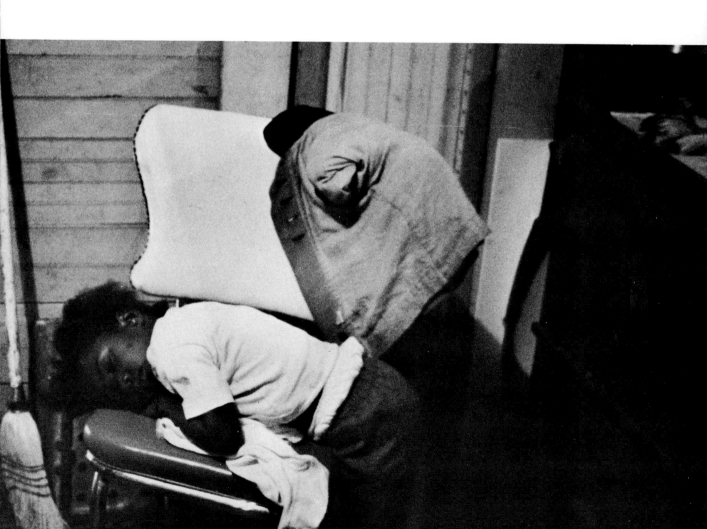

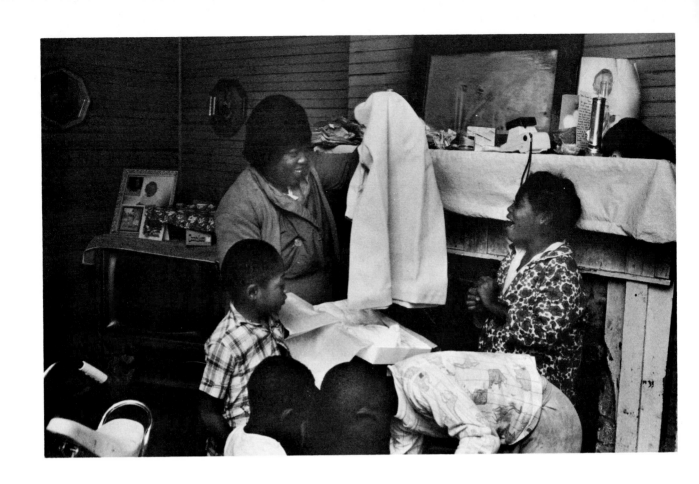

Christmas morning we all got up very early. Junior woke up first, and then he woke me up saying, "Sweet Pea, it's Christmas!" We all went into the front room — and there were so many bikes that we could hardly fit in!

Mama saved all year to buy wheels for us, and Rodney and Joanne got a new swing set. I got a pocketbook and a comb and a brush and a dress and some socks and slippers and panties and a slip. The dress was my favorite present because it's yellow and that's my favorite color.

It was the very best Christmas we've ever had.

I felt happy all day.

This book is dedicated
with love
and
with thanks
to Sweet Pea's family
and to her friends